RED DUST, DIAMOND SKY

Suzanne Cass

To my dad, who loves the bush.

Roses for Maude

There was close to one million dollars scattered on the floor around him. Nine hundred and eighty two thousand three hundred and forty dollars, to be exact.

George considered the cash placed in haphazard piles covering most of his dusty living room floor.

It was close to daybreak and he was too tired to think anymore. He'd make a decision about the money in the morning. Right now he needed sleep.

Grabbing hold of the edge of the battered wooden table, he used it to lever himself off the floor. His sixty-year-old bones protested loudly as he rose, slow as a tortoise, to standing. The floorboards creaked nearly as loudly beneath his socked feet as he went around turning off the lights. He pulled the chain on the musty brown reading lamp next to his favourite armchair. Gosh that chair had seen some years—nearly as many as he had—but it was still the most comfortable thing he'd ever sat in. Almost reminded him of the times Jill would wrap her arms around him and laugh into his neck, telling him she loved him, even if he did smell like sheep-dip.

He missed Jill. She would've known what to do with this mess he'd got himself into tonight.

He headed towards the hallway, reaching for the greying switch on the wall that would douse the bare bulb swinging overhead. Fingers suspended over the switch he noticed the brown paper packets sitting in an innocent mound next to the threadbare couch. His stomach contracted. He'd decide what to do with *those* tomorrow too.

Lying down in bed with a grunt of gratitude he pulled the blanket up to his chin and closed his eyes. But sleep wouldn't come. Instead his mind kept wandering back over tonight's events.

It'd started out much as any other night; him and Blue out rambling through the night, breathing in the stars, relishing the crunch of red earth beneath his feet. George wasn't much of a sleeper, not since Jill died anyway. Instead of whiling away his sleepless hours cooped up inside, he and his red kelpie, Blue, would patrol through the night-time countryside. Checking on his sheep, or testing the air for signs of rain.

But tonight, instead of only the pale starlight to illuminate each stalk of grass, make the trees stand out like dark watchmen, there'd been the flash of bright lights away in the distance. And deep male voices breaking through the soft chirp of the crickets.

By the time George made his way over the grassy rolling rise and dip of the pasture, a car started up. It's headlights flooded the surrounding stand of white gums, igniting them like spectres in the night. Then a large ute sped away, spewing a hazy dust trail behind it.

George always carried his trusty torch with him.

And of course he needed to investigate.

He found a pathetic attempt by ... whoever it was, to cover up the fact they'd just dug a big hole behind an overturned stump by untidily brushing leaves and branches over the top of the mound.

Jesus Mary Mother of God. Chills ran down his spine. Was he about to stumble on a buried body?

He hesitated, the torch held in a trembling hand sending out dancing flickers of light. He should call the police. That's what he should do. Jill always said he was as curious as a cat. Or was it curiosity killed the cat? Whatever it was, he wasn't leaving until he knew for sure. He found a long stick and started to dig up the ground.

And now there was nearly a million dollars and a stash of drugs in his living room.

* * *

George stood studying his handiwork. A trickle of sweat ran between his shoulder blades. It was only mid-morning but the day was already turning into another blue-sky scorcher. There was a flat area of newly dug earth partially hidden behind the stand of old paperbarks near the fence line, right on the farthest boundary of his farm. His tractor huffed a little smoke cloud as it sat idling nearby. He'd make sure not to let the sheep in here for a while. Who knew if that horrible drug, ice—and he was pretty sure that's what it was, he'd seen enough of it on telly lately—could leach through the soil and into the pasture, but he wasn't about to take any chances.

Throwing one more glance over his shoulder at the now quiet earth, he climbed back up onto his tractor and headed towards the homestead. A tuneless whistle erupted from between his lips. It was a wonder how much lighter he felt now that filthy stuff was gone and buried. Those bloody drug lords, or whoever they were, would be in for a big surprise when they came back to dig up their booty. His whistle got louder.

Drug pushers were the scourge of the Earth. The thought stopped him mid-toot. His hands gripped the wheel of the tractor tighter. Just look at what that drug had done to poor Sandy Morecombe's boy, Daniel. Died of an overdose. They found him lying by the road up behind the truck stop on Mair Street.

And Sasha Symore and Tye Rogers, both of them in jail for theft and aggravated assault. They said they'd needed money to pay for more drugs. Sasha's parents had packed up their belongings, sold their farm and moved to the city, so they could be near her, help her get clean again once she got out of jail.

More and more young people of this town were being sucked in by the insidious nature of ice. Including Flynn.

George still couldn't believe Flynn was involved with the stuff. His son had an addiction to ice. It was so very hard to admit. Addiction. Such a terrible thing. Almost impossible to break. For the millionth time, George wondered what he'd done wrong; what he could've done differently. Flynn was in the city now, wouldn't come home no matter how much George begged. George hadn't spoken to him in months, wasn't even sure where he was. How he was doing. He resisted the urge to beat his fist on the steering wheel.

One thing was for sure, those blasted drug dealers weren't going to get their money back. They weren't likely to go crying to the cops once they discovered the theft either. And he hadn't come down in the last shower of rain, he'd keep it hidden, safe. No one would guess where it'd gone.

The whistle returned of its own accord. Bouncing gently in the tractor seat, he enjoyed the feel of the sunshine pounding on his back.

Maybe later he'd pop in and see how Maude was doing. Go and see if that damn hospital had moved her up the waiting list for her hip replacement yet. It was doing her head in having to wait so long and her wonderful garden was suffering because she couldn't get out into it anymore. Maude was Jill's best friend. He still liked to go and have a cup of tea and a friendly chat with her every now and then, even though it'd been six years since Jill had passed. He liked to see Maude smile; it made his heart feel lighter somehow.

* * *

'Can I get you a beer?'

'Thanks, Jimmy, that'd be great.' George smiled as he took a seat at a small table next to the pub window. He cast his gaze around the interior, nodding at a couple of other mates sitting over near the pool table. It was early evening and he'd decided to stop in for one quick drink after his shopping expedition in town. Stocking up on essentials. His kitchen cupboards had become decidedly bare recently. He'd been a little preoccupied over the past few months, since he'd dug up all that money.

Within a few minutes Jimmy returned with two large schooners, beads of condensation swimming down the outside of the glass.

'Jeez, it was hot today, huh?' said George as he wrapped a large fist around the glass.

'Yeah, it was.' Jimmy waved the question away with a flapping hand. 'But have you heard about the bloody community hall though, George?' Jimmy's tufted eyebrows nearly disappeared into his non-existent hairline. George felt a prickle of sweat break out on his forehead and he took a long swallow of beer.

When he didn't' reply, Jimmy jumped in again. 'It looks bloody fantastic. Have you seen it? Brand spanking new paint job on the outside and all the floors sanded and varnished inside as well.' Jimmy crossed his arms and sat back on his stool. George took another swig and absorbed his words.

'Wow, that's ... wonderful. So the shire finally shelled out, huh?' George wouldn't meet his friend's eyes.

'No. That's the mystery of the whole bloody thing.' Jimmy lowered his voice in a conspiratorial manner. 'The mayor is saying they never sanctioned any such thing.' Jimmy leaned forward and let go his hold on his glass to wave his hands around in the air again. George sat back, away from Jimmy's enthusiasm and took another long drink. 'There was a bit of confusion for a while, the mayor thought that the local CWA had organised it. And then they thought maybe someone had applied for a government grant to get it done. But no one's taking credit for it. They're blaming some bloody anonymous benefactor.' Jimmy blew out a breath and grabbed his beer as if it were a life preserver. 'Whaddya think of that?'

'I ... I think it's great,' George replied. 'That hall has needed a revamp for years ... No, decades now. It might even lift morale a little around here. God knows Smokey Ridge could do with a dose of good luck. Does it really matter who did it?'

'Well, I guess if you put it that way ...' Jimmy seemed lost for words. But his silence was only momentary. 'And what about old Sam Becket, over at the Black Bush property.' Jimmy was leaning forward again. George reached for his beer and was surprised to find the glass empty. 'Old Sam's been going around telling everyone who'll listen that two days after his bloody tractor packed it in—which might've been the last straw according to Sam, he might've just up and sold after that because everything's been going from bad to worse over there—well he found a shiny new tractor parked in his shed when he woke up that morning. With a note saying it was a present from a friend.'

'Now that does sound a little odd,' George agreed, swiping at his sweaty brow.

'That's not all though, there's been other stuff happening round here. Things being mysteriously fixed. And the road out to Curalgalan? It was bloody graded a few weeks ago. Imagine that,' Jimmy continued.

Standing up quickly, almost knocking the stool over, George said, 'Good to catch up with you Jim, but I gotta go. Things to do on the farm, you know.' Placing his trusty hat on his head he strode out of the pub. Taking a few steadying breaths, he started his ute and took off down Main Street.

On a whim, he turned onto one of the side streets that meandered back around the outskirts of Smokey Ridge. Slowing down, he craned his neck to look at number twenty-two as he drove by. The garden looked immaculate once more. The little lavender hedges were neatly trimmed, the grass was green and manicured, and bright flowers poked their heads out in the flowerbeds. And there was Maud, sitting on her front porch, a small smile playing over her face as she gazed over her yard. He kept driving, not wanting to stop, still rattled by Jimmy's talk. He just needed to get home. But he was glad Maude looked happy. She'd told him last week when he'd popped in to see her that Dave from Mr Lawns and Gardens was coming in once a week now. And that Dave had told Maude someone had paid him—by leaving a large envelope of cash in his letterbox, which was a most foolhardy thing to do if you asked Dave—to look after her place for a whole year. Wasn't it just wonderful, she'd said with a smile.

* * *

'You need to update your furniture, Dad. This stuff's as ancient as the hills.' Flynn's gaze shifted around the lounge room. George just grinned. 'And for God's sake, spend some money on a lick of paint for the walls. I'll even help you if you like. This poor old house needs a bit of TLC.' George's grin got even broader. His son was back. Had just appeared on the front veranda one morning about a month ago. George didn't ask and Flynn didn't tell. It was as simple as that. But George knew one thing for sure, his son was clean again. Almost back to his old self once more.

'So, when does Uni start?' George asked, handing Flynn a ham and cheese sandwich on a plate.

They both clanged through the rickety fly-screen door and

took a seat out on the veranda before Flynn answered. 'The last week in February, so I've still got plenty of time left to give you a hand painting the house.'

'That'd be nice, thanks, Flynn.' That left him three whole more weeks to spend with his son. Heaven.

'I still can't believe I won that scholarship to Uni,' his son said conversationally, staring out over the brown paddocks. 'I always thought they were pretty hard to get.'

'I wouldn't worry about that. You deserve it. You deserve to be able to get an education, like everyone else. That money's yours, it's going to help you get back on your feet. Now tell me, what is Cyber Engineering again?'

* * *

Life was funny sometimes. George had often wondered what he'd do if he ever won a million dollars in the lottery. Dreamed about how he'd spend the money. Now Smokey Ridge was a township that could hold it's head high once more. Small changes often made a big difference.

Lifting the corner of the mattress, George counted one hundred and thirty three dollars. The very last of it. Perhaps he could invite Maude out to dinner. They might go to the local RSL club for a steak and chips, or maybe a chicken schnitzel. There might even be enough money left over to buy Maude a bunch of roses. Perhaps it was time. He'd been on his own for six years now. Jill would understand.

Leaving his Mark

'I think I've found it.' Jordan turned towards the voice that drifted over on an arid gust of wind.

'Where are you?' He peered through the scrubby Mallee bush to pinpoint exactly where his father, Tom, had called from.

'Over here. Walk towards the bluff, I've found a little clearing.' Jordan swatted at the interminable flies buzzing around his face as he traipsed through the ochre dirt. Dry, scratchy bushes hindered his path, and he pushed and grunted until he suddenly stumbled into a clearing. There was his dad standing in front of a huge desert oak. Leaves as sparse and spiky as a cactus, the old tree was tall, towering over the thirsty landscape as it clung tenaciously to life.

'This is it,' his father exclaimed. 'I can hardly believe we found it.' Jordan went over to where his father was running a hand gently over the damaged bark. 'The old surveyors mark,' Tom murmured. 'I chiselled this blaze.' His finger traced the weathered writing on the wooden plaque, cut into a flat section of the tree where a strip of bark had been removed. 'Look, here's the benchmark too.' Tom kicked unsteadily at the red earth with a dusty boot and partially uncovered a lump of grey concrete at the base of the tree. 'We used the desert oaks because not much kills 'em, and the bark doesn't grow over our hand-cut shields.'

Jordan stared at his father's craggy face. Sparse grey hair floated around his almost bald pate. Eyes, once a vivacious hazel, now a murky brown, were distant, lost in another time and another place. Pursed lips curled into a hint of a smile. A completely different man from four weeks ago stood in front of Jordan now. Calm. Fulfilled. Four weeks ago his father's face had still been craggy and eroded, but it'd also been drab, creased with loneliness and worry about his declining health. All the light extinguished, gone from those once expressive eyes. But now? A renaissance had taken place. The confident, capable, man-of-few-words with an ever-ready smile Jordan remembered from his childhood was re-emerging.

Jordan's memory flipped back to the day, a month ago, when he'd sat next to Tom on the battered brown sofa in his shadowed living room.

'What have you got there, Dad?' Jordan had taken the photo gently from his father's gnarled fingers. It was shot of a dusty orange Land Rover, cresting the wave of a sand dune, the scraggly desert unfurling into the distance behind it. Four young men stood around on the sand, eyes trained on far horizons, faces unlined and eager.

Jordan flipped the photo, the thick card uneven beneath his fingertips. A faint date was scrawled in a scratchy hand, *25 Oct 1960.*

'That's me,' his dad said, holding up a hand for the photo and pointing to a figure on the far right.

'Wow. You look so … young. And happy.'

'That's because I was.' Jordan's chest squeezed tight at his father's simple words.

'Where did you get it?' he asked, avoiding the sooty black cloud of despair that hung between them.

'It fell out the back of this.' Tom held up a battered leather photo album. The one he'd been half-heartedly flicking through, while Jordan sat in silence and pretended to be interested. But really he'd been nursing thoughts about his redundancy and how long the small amount of money would keep him going before he found another job. He still had all the lawyers fees left to pay from the messy divorce. They couldn't be put off any longer.

His hand clenched into a fist on the armrest of the corduroy sofa.

There wasn't much else that could go wrong. His life had gone from being so, so busy, to suddenly … Nothing … A blank page.

What to do with that blank page? So many possibilities. But none that appealed.

His focus returned to his father. A troubled reflection of the man he'd once been. Jordan tried to pinpoint exactly when his dad had flipped from a happy, confident man in his prime, to the sad specimen in front of him now. Was it after Mum died? His mind struggled to go back a decade or so and filter through all the images of Tom then. But he couldn't recall the specifics; all he remembered was his own efficient determination to get the family through his mother's funeral and then move on with life. He hadn't paid enough attention. Certainly not to his father.

Tom still held the photo in precarious fingers, but he wasn't looking at it, instead he stared out the window. Jordan's attention went to the photo of his father looking so happy.

'C'mon, dad, let's go and get you packed. We're going on a trip.' Jordan slapped his knee and stood up.

'Where?' Tom's voice was thin and hesitant. 'I can't leave my house.'

'Your house will be fine for a few weeks. We're going outback. We might even find that old survey tree you keep telling me about.' He wasn't taking no for an answer. His dad needed something. They both needed something.

Every day since he'd uttered those words had been a revelation.

The first few days in the car, heading west, had been hard. Tom was uncertain and frail, sullen and quick to disagree with everything Jordan did and said. Child-like in his total dependence on Jordan.

Jordan loaded up his late model 4WD with all the camping gear he could rustle up. Enough to see them through four weeks in the outback. The only holidays they'd ever done as a family—back when his mum was alive and he was a gangling teen who only wanted to stay at home and sit in front of the telly—were camping trips to National Parks, both near and far. He'd protested and scorned those trips, sulked most of the time, but now he knew those skills he'd need to survive a trip into the desert were there somewhere, rusty and long forgotten, but there.

He'd also spent hours talking to doctors and nurses and specialists about his father's medical needs. There was no more chemo or radiotherapy that could cure him, the cancer had spread too far. It was all just about time now. This trip was about quality, not quantity.

Slowly, as the miles unfolded before them, the blacktop of bitumen leading them further and further into their dream, Tom started to loosen up, unfurl and remember. At first there'd been odd little snippets of information, dropped into the otherwise long silences for Jordan to decipher. But as the hot wind coiled through the open windows of the car and the years of antipathy and loss finally dropped away, Jordan started to formulate the story of his father's life.

Tom had been part of a survey team employed to transfer levels from the east of Australia to the west. Jordan was amazed to find out that the sea level on the east coast was frequently different to the level on the west coast. He'd always assumed sea level was the same wherever you went. The transects his father had done went towards forming a grid of levels for seismic readings covering the whole of Australia, to finally bring about a base line for height surveys in the future.

Tom told tales of how his group of young, carefree men, laden down with theodolites, star-pickets, bags of concrete, canvas tents, swags, cooking gear and lots and lots of tinned spam, headed off into one of the most isolated parts of the world. How they—as the junior surveyors—were only allocated the orange soft-top Land Rovers that leaked when it rained and let the all-pervasive red dust filter in around the edges, while the senior surveyors were allowed the luxury of driving the grey hard-tops.

It sounded like a harsh existence, spending months and months in the desolate, dry bush, where they could go weeks without even seeing a cloud. But the more he listened to his father, the more he got the inkling it was really about the camaraderie, the challenge of living rough, the joy of watching a sunrise, pink and demure over a flat, barren wilderness. The sheer beauty of it all tearing at his father's soul. That kind of thing could never be forgotten. Or replaced.

Something Jordan had never experienced in his mad headlong rush to be the best he could at everything. His job, his marriage, his children, everything was pigeonholed and dealt with competently and quickly. And all of a sudden he was envious of his father and the life he'd lived.

A few days ago, while still navigating through the Northern Territory, they'd followed a rutted dirt track around the base of a jutting rock spire—from a distance it was a band of granite and sandstone that ran only slightly higher than the rest of the flat landscape, ending in an abrupt cliff face, as if some almighty God had sliced it off with a knife. But once they arrived beneath the cliff face it towered high above them.

Tom pointed. 'That's Mt Leisler. We used this area as a base for a while. Even set up a camp kitchen here.' Jordan remembered a photo depicting grey canvas tents flapping in a hot breeze and a camp stove set up over an open fire where they'd cooked a whole lamb they'd haggled from the local stockmen.

'I remember one day we came across this group of aboriginals. We'd stopped to get water at Purtardi Springs.' Tom never looked at Jordan when he spoke, he preferred to stare out the open window at the marching red sands. 'They were all as naked as the day they were born. And black as the ace of spades.' Tom laughed. 'We were probably the first white folks they'd ever seen.'

'Wow. That's amazing, Dad.' It was hard to imagine in this modern, fast-paced world, that it hadn't been so long ago when this might've been commonplace.

'The women and kids were friendly enough, even though they couldn't understand much of what we said, but the buck, he just stood off to one side leaning on his spear and stared at us. No doubt they were wondering what the hell we were up to,' his dad said with a soft smile. 'We left them a battered billy to carry water in. Not much else we could give them, really. Not much else they needed.'

The further they travelled the more the stories leaked from Tom. His voice became stronger with every day they spent in the desert, his back a little straighter. They crossed from the Northern Territory into Western Australia, and now, today, they found the blaze tree. It was a good day.

Soon they'd finish this trip, and then reality would come creeping back in. His dad would go back to his decaying house and Jordan would go back to his small, empty apartment. The kids were at University now; they only stayed with him when they needed a place to crash for the night. He tried not to think about it as he set up camp in the evening glow. They found a lovely bush camp, just off the main track, with a hand-operated bore pump for water, but otherwise no facilities. He was fine with that. They had the place to themselves and after Jordan set up the two little tents and got the small gas stove fired up for a cuppa, he took the camp chairs to the top of the highest sand dune.

'Dad, come up here,' he hollered. His dad was knee deep in the spinifex at the bottom of the dune, head tipped back to stare at the sky. Tom turned and shuffled slowly up the slope. Jordan's first instinct might've been to go and offer his dad an arm to lean on. But he knew better. His dad was regaining his independence, his self-respect, his delight in the small things, and he'd be dammed if he were going to take that away from him now.

'I thought we might watch the sunset from up here,' Jordan said, indicating one of the chairs when Tom finally made it to the top. He handed the old man a hot cup of tea and took the other chair.

'I'd like that,' replied Tom, blowing the steam from the top of his mug. They sat in companionable silence, watching the sun sink in the west. The land and sky morphed together, blurred at the edges, the colours slowly changing from fiery orange, to russet to deepening indigo. The red dust faded into the diamond sky. A flock of pink and greys flew across the desert, low and erratic, their faint screeches spiralling up to meet the sunset.

Jordan had meant this trip to be a re-living of his father's memories. But today—this trip—had brought the past and the present crashing together. They couldn't really be extricated from one another. And Jordan knew things had to change.

'When we get home, I'm going to come and live with your

for a while. Okay, Dad?'

   'I'd like that,' his father replied, still staring at the sunset.

Solar Flare

Tipping her head back, Lissa let the sunlight flow over her. Not caring that the touch of the sun's rays would add to the smattering of freckles already adorning her features, she delighted in the warmth stroking her cheeks. Opening her eyes, she took in the simple endless blue above.

How she loved the sun. It'd taken some getting used to, the merciless sunshine that hounded her all day. But now, after seven weeks, she was becoming familiar with the terrible heat of the West Australian outback.

The animal beneath her writhed, bringing her awareness back to the dusty yard.

'Lissa, watch what you're doin!'

She gave an involuntary start at Barry's loud reprimand.

'Sorry, boss.' Blowing a lock of flaming auburn hair out of her eyes, she tightened her grip on the calf's front leg, leaning all the weight into her right knee to hold down its bony head. The calf rolled the whites of its eyes, naïve and terrified. It let out a muffled bellow, raising a plume of dust from the ground with its breath. Lissa agreed with the sentiment behind the calf's cry. Branding was a disturbing, painful experience.

'Orright, let 'im go.'

Lissa leapt up, watching the calf scramble for a footing,

raising a choking red cloud as it found its feet and took off towards the cattle-yard fence.

'Only a few more to go, hey?' Barry let out a loud, belly-shaking whoop. Lissa raised a tight smile.

'Aww, come on kid, it aint that bad.' He gave a sly waggle of one of his bushy eyebrows and she had to smile back. Barry had taken a little getting used to as well, but now she found the leading station hand was growing on her. 'Well, go and grab another one then,' he said, turning his back to ready the branding iron for the next calf.

'I'll give you a hand, if you like.'

Lissa whipped her head around at the unexpected closeness of the deep, masculine voice. Ace. His dimple wreathed grin made her forget for a second exactly where she was. Lost for words, she stared up at him. God, he was tall. Even, taller than her, and not many men could say that. Watching her from beneath the brim of his hat, he eventually raised an arm and pointed towards the bawling bundle of calves in the adjoining yard.

'You know, with the calves.'

'Sure,' she stammered. Following him towards the holding yard, she watched his long jean-clad legs stride out, his faded cowboy boots scuffing through the dust. Ace was the station owner's youngest son. The very gorgeous youngest son. Of course she'd noticed him. She'd noticed him the very first day she'd taken the job on this isolated cattle station. But she was just one of the many hired hands to drift through the peripheries of his life. She could count the number of times she'd spoken to him on one hand. Now here he was, offering her his help.

Ace chose their next victim and together they dragged the bucking tangle of brown hide into the middle of the yard and wrangled it to the ground in front of Barry. Lissa knelt in the dirt next to Ace, close, almost touching him. She could feel his proximity through the cotton of her shirt. She inhaled the heady scent of heat and dust; and something else. Him. It was him she could smell, a mixture of sweat and sunbeams and musky leather.

'How long you been out here now?' He was trying to make conversation. Her mouth felt dry. Talking to guys was not one of her strong points, especially not good-looking ones who stared at her with an air of expectance.

'It'll be two months on Friday.' She brushed several of the ever-present flies away from her face.

'Worked up north before?'

She shook her head.

'You don't say much do you?' He shot another of his winning grins in her direction. 'You're different from the rest.'

She opened her mouth to tell him it wasn't true when the calf gave a desperate heave, and her words were lost in a grunt as she struggled to control the animal.

'Nice necklace,' Ace said, once the calf was still again, his gaze dropping to the opening V of her shirt.

'Thanks,' she replied, reaching up to touch it reflexively. 'It's a sunstone pendant.'

'That's a good name for it. It's got all the colours of the sun in there.'

'Yeah ... I got it when I was living in Melbourne. They don't get too much sunshine down there,' she added.

He studied Lissa through side-slanted eyes. 'Well, it's nice. It matches your hair.'

Was he flirting with her?

Ace brought his gaze up from her pendant and let his eyes rest on her face. *Outstanding eyes.* The abstract thought made her blink in surprise. Where had that come from? Even if he did have glorious rich chocolate eyes that reminded her of her grandmother's fudge brownies, he was off limits. Wasn't' he?

One morning, a few days after she arrived, she'd been struggling to saddle one of the horses when Ace had appeared as if from nowhere, offering assistance. But no sooner had he lifted the saddle out of her arms than his father, the station owner, appeared and commanded Ace come and give him a hand. As they'd walked away, Lissa overheard his father talking to Ace in a low, stern voice about his responsibilities on the farm, and how they *didn't* include flirting with any of the seasonal stock hands. Ace argued that it was all just harmless, but his father stalled him with a dismissive wave of his hand and walked away, leaving Ace glowering at his back.

Yep, he was definitely off limits.

Before she could think of an answer to his intriguing comment, Barry said, 'Orright, let 'im go,' and they set off to drag another calf over.

'You know, you remind me of an old pocket watch I used to have, it always ticked and the hands always went around and around like they should, but it never did show the exact right time.' His fingers brushed over hers as they grappled together for the next frightened calf. His touch left a burning trail over her skin, the tingling heat flowing up her arm and into her body.

'Really? Are you saying I'm broken?' She allowed her teeth to show in a smile, to hide the fact he caused such a reaction in her.

'No, that's not what I meant.' He stumbled over the words. 'You're not broken. Just ... unusual. You seem to like your own company.'

'Is there anything wrong with that?'

'No, not at all.'

She could still feel the texture of his hands on her skin.

'I'm not trying to be rude. I'm just not much of a conversationalist,' she said, shrugging her acceptance of her self-proclaimed flaw.

'That's okay, I can talk enough for the both of us,' he replied, wading into the milling throng of brown and tan hides. She took the chance to inspect his tall, lean frame, noticing the muscles of his shoulder flexing beneath the material of his t-shirt. He was the complete package, good-looking, hardworking, with the backing of a rich family. Surely he had a girlfriend? They were probably lining up from all over the district.

Snaffling up a passing calf, he caught it without effort in strong arms. She watched his biceps bulge as the calf kicked half-heartedly and then he straightened, staring at her.

'Why don't we have a drink one night, and I'll prove I can do witty repartee when I want to.' The words spilled from her mouth before she could stop them.

'All right then. I'll come tonight. And I'll bring the beer.' He grappled with the back of the calf, Lissa belatedly grabbing the front legs and helping him carry it over to Barry.

'Sure,' she answered, kneeling on the ground next to the calf. *Shit.* What had she just done?

Waiting for Barry and the branding iron, Lissa let her gaze drift to the horizon, blurring into distance with an absence of defined borders. If the city had been her cage then the desert was her liberty. Ever since she'd left Melbourne after her father died a year ago, it was as if a terrible weight had lifted from her shoulders. She'd thrown her meagre possessions into the back of her battered yellow ute, and escaped, letting the bitumen take her where it wanted, seeking the sun wherever she went.

The resonant warble of a magpie reawakened her awareness and she dropped her gaze back to the dusty yard. And now the sun had led her here. To this cattle station in the outback. To where Ace crouched beside her, his nearness setting the tiny hairs on her arm standing up to attention. Her heart gave a surprising kick beneath her ribs when she thought about this gorgeous man who wanted to have a beer with her.

* * *

Ace tapped on the door to her cabin, the sound reverberating through the evening sky. What the hell was he doing here? He almost turned on his heel and walked away, but then he heard her say, 'Hi Ace.' Sweeping the door open, she let it clang back on its metal hinges. Tonight her curves were softened by a long, flowing skirt that swished across the floor, her fiery hair loose, long strands flying around her round face. Did she know how gorgeous she looked, standing there, hands on hips, framed by the open door?

'Beer,' he said, holding up a six-pack, offering her a genuine smile. He was here, he couldn't back out now.

'Thanks. Shall we go sit round the back?' She was nervous, he could tell by the slight quaver in her voice. Her nerves were echoed in his own churning stomach. But his nerves were more from the thought of what his father would say if he found out he was here. Ace withstood the urge to cast a quick glance over his shoulder.

'Sounds good.' He followed her through the tiny cabin and out the back door. Outside there was an array of mismatched chairs to choose from. The air still held heat from the late afternoon sun's rays and the air chimed with the sounds of frogs calling from the nearby tank stand.

'What's that?' Ace indicated the strange shape, all odd angles and long legs, reminiscent of an intoxicated spider.

'It's a solar telescope. I like to look at the sun.' Was that a defensive hitch he heard in her tone?

He strolled over to the contraption and placed a hand on the smooth metallic surface. 'Can I take a look?'

'Sure, go ahead.' She gestured towards the telescope. 'There're supposed to be some great solar flares erupting today. I've got it trained on a large sunspot—that's the darker spot you can see on the surface,' she said, her hands moving in an enthusiastic dance. It was the most animated he'd ever seen her. As she talked, her cheeks flushed pink as a rose, and he found himself not really listening to the rest of what she was saying, instead fighting the urge to run a finger down the curve of her creamy cheek. Would her skin be as soft as it looked? He'd wanted to find out the answer to that question from the very first day she'd walked into the machinery shed. Even though her clothes had been creased and dishevelled from her five-hour drive to reach the isolated homestead and her red hair escaping from her ponytail was all wispy and knotted, he'd noticed her pale beauty. And those sombre grey eyes. Eyes that held mysteries, hidden behind her reserved gaze.

Lissa wasn't a conventional beauty. She was tall, nearly as tall as him, her curves generous, with full round breasts and long legs. Nothing like the slim hipped, small breasted women, with easy smiles and self-confident charm he was usually drawn to. His father would give Lissa her marching orders without a second thought if he knew what Ace was doing tonight. Fraternising with the station hands was against his father's rules. She wasn't good enough for his youngest son. Lissa was a drifter, with no true home, no money, no connections, searching for something intangible. An outsider. Ace was expected to marry into outback aristocracy, find a good wife, with good breeding, who understood how things worked in this harsh country.

But in the past few weeks, Ace found himself instinctively drawn to Lissa's presence, watching for her in the stock yards before they mounted up for a day of mustering, or studying her out of the corner of his eye as she stood, kicking up the ochre dust with the rest of the station hands at smoko, drinking billy tea. Then he would catch a glimpse of her red hair caught in the sun's rays, and it was like a match flaring in the dark recesses of his soul. He'd fought his involuntary inclinations, turning away from her every time she came near. And yet, look where he found himself now. As if his legs had walked themselves over to Lissa's cottage of their own volition.

'Sorry, what did you say?' he apologised, leaning forward and looking through the eyepiece, hoping to hide his discomfit at being caught out not listening. Wow, the vista through the viewfinder was amazing, intense fiery colours assaulted his eyes.

'My dad gave it to me, just before he died.' The statement was quiet, a breath of wind blowing through the evening air.

'Oh.' Ace could feel the weight behind her words. He kept staring though the ocular lens, watching the luminescent orange surface of the sun curve through the plane of his vision, so bright it almost hurt his eyes.

'You miss your dad?' The statement was a foreign one for him. His father was a hard man, shaped by the tough realities of eking out a living from the land, the pressure of constant droughts and dust and cattle prices. The kind of man Ace knew he didn't ever want to become.

'Yeah.' She was silent for long enough that he finally looked up from the telescope to see her standing close to him, her fingers touching the small pendant which rested in the hollow of her throat. 'He gave me this pendant. He said it would give me courage and independence.'

'Sunstones must be rare. I've never seen one before. It's beautiful.' *Like you.* He had to force the words back down his throat. On impulse he reached up and took the necklace between his fingers, to feel the weight of the alien stone. The dying rays of the sun caught it, making it shimmer and glow, as if from a hidden source of light within. The movement brought him closer to her. He could see a tiny vein in her neck, beating along with the tattoo of her heart. Prickles of sensation ran beneath his skin, a feeling cf recognition.

Rearranging his facial muscles into the semblance of a smile he said, 'I reckon these sunstones might be the closest th ng to magic I've ever seen.'

'I think so too.' She touched his hand. A fleeting brush of her fingertips over his palm as he played with the sunstone. Then she gave a coaxing laugh. 'That's one of the reasons I wanted to come and work in the outback. Everything in the sky is so bright and alive, as if it's going to jump down the telescope at me.' Her long skirt brushed the ground, making a whispering sound. 'And because of the kind of people I've met out here.' Her eyes narrowed ever so slightly. She wasn't laughing now, the lines on her face smooth, her plump lips parted and fascinating. The hot evening air felt still, the silence clinging like a shroud.

He wanted to kiss her. The urge flowed through him like an unstoppable wave. He closed his eyes against the craving.

'Are you okay?' she asked, her soft voice washing over him. He managed to open his eyes again. They were standing so close, her pendant still resting in his fingers.

Sure, never been better, he wanted to say, but the words wouldn't come. He wanted to back away from her, dismiss her with a flippant wave of his hand. But he'd underestimated Lissa and the effect she had on him. It was unfair, the ease of how she burrowed her way into his awareness. Into his heart and soul.

'You're a fascinating woman, Lissa.' The five words seemed to form echoes of themselves, rebounding back to his ears over and over again. She grinned, her rosy cheeks alight with surprise. His father was going to hate this.

Ace leaned in and let his lips graze hers.

'Oh ...' she whispered, her mouth moving beneath his. But she didn't back away. In fact she did the opposite. Her hand snaked up to rest at the nape of his neck, gently, inexorably pulling him in, letting the pressure of her lips increase until he was kissing her long, and deep and slow. Lissa was so warm and welcoming and alive, and he wanted her more than any other woman before. He was baffled by the change that was taking place inside him—in his heart. And in that moment he knew he would do anything, go anywhere, give up everything to be with her.

Other Books by this Author

Chasing Bullets

He'd die for her.

Island Redemption

Who will win at the game of love?

Glass Clouds

Her survival depends on a dangerous stranger.

Shadows in the Dust

Peril and passion in the Outback.

Suzanne Cass

Connect with the Author

I really hope you enjoyed reading Red Dust, Diamond Sky. For more action romance info and upcoming release dates, sign up for my latest newsletter. As an added bonus, you'll get a copy of my FREE BOOK.

Rain on a Tin Roof

Will her reluctant hero turn out to be the man of her dreams?

Or you can stay in touch via my website
www.suzannecass.com

Or

The greatest gift you could ever give an author is to leave a review. You will be helping other people to discover this book and making a difference to me as an Independently Published Author. If you liked this book and want other people to read it to, please leave a review.

About the Author

Suzanne Cass has always had a fascination with the tough resilience of people who live in our amazing red-dirt country of Australia. Much of her adolescence was spent working as a jillaroo in the Snowy Mountains, forming her love of enigmatic, outback heroes in wild, passionate, dangerous stories. When not writing about the characters inhabiting her head, Suzanne can be found roaming the Perth beaches with her border collie, or encouraging her two sons from the sidelines as they play their respective sports.